PART ONE

CAR TRAVEL GAMES

Tony Potter

Edited by Jenny Tyler

Designed by Tony Potter

Illustrated by Iain Ashman and Chris Lyon

Additional illustrations by Guy Smith

2 Playing travel games
4 Journey log
6 Games and puzzles
30 Answers

Playing travel games

There are lots of games, puzzles and activities in this book. Some can be played on your own, but others are for teams. More than one person is needed whenever you see this picture symbol:

You can score points in lots of the games. You might like to make a score card, like the one shown on the right, so that you can see who is the overall winner at the end of a journey. It is a good idea to ask one person to keep the scores and be referee. The referee is in charge and decides how many points each person scores. Games with scores have this picture symbol:

It helps to have a pencil and paper handy for some of the games and puzzles. These are essential when you see this picture symbol:

Most of the games can be altered to suit your journey. For example, there are lists of things to spot which you can change to suit motorway rather than town driving.

You can play many of the games and solve the puzzles at home. Some have special rules to follow if you want to do this.

You will find answers to all the puzzles on pages 30 to 32.

It is very dangerous for drivers to take their eyes off the road. They can join in some games safely, but may not want to play at all, so it is best not to bother them by keep asking. Try not to distract the driver by moving about or making too much noise.

GAME	AUNTY ETHEL	SPIKE (THE DOG)	GRUMPY GRANDPA	ME
Collector's quest	10	8	9	10
Zoo	10	0	0	0
Navigator	5	5	0	0
Missing parts	3	3	2	12
Memory car	12	10	5	10
TOTAL	40	26	16	32

WINNER: Aunty Ethel ← with help from me

For some games you might find it helpful for each person to keep a tally of their score, like this:

1 Draw a line for each point scored, up to four, like this: ||||

2 Then draw another line to show you have five points, like this: ||||

3 Carry on scoring in chunks of five points. This makes it easy to add the scores at the end of the game.

|||| ||||
|||| ||||
||| = 23

Things to take

You need to take these things with you to be able to play the games. It is a good idea to read this book before leaving, as there are some things to make which are easier to do at home.

Log book (see page 5)

Tear off notepad

Your scorecard

Something to write with.

Watch

Maps of your journey

Things you have made from the book to bring.

Blu-tack (Trade name for a sticky putty-like substance.)

Here are some other things you might like to pack in your bag to take with you.

Newspaper to see what's on the car radio.

Plastic bags for collecting things in.

Drink

Guide books

Calculator

Pencil sharpener. Don't make your pencils too sharp, or you might hurt yourself if the car stops suddenly.

Rubber

Torch

Compass

Things to do before leaving

You could ask the driver if you can help with anything before leaving. This picture shows some things you may be able to do.

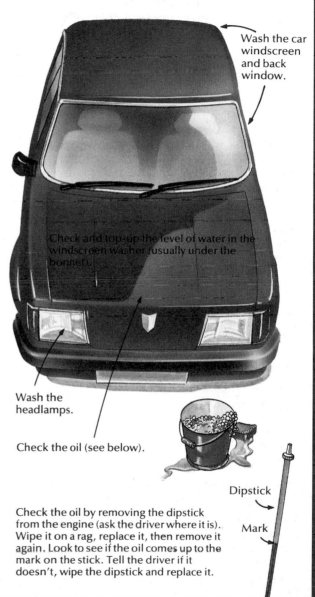

Wash the car windscreen and back window.

Check and top-up the level of water in the windscreen washer (usually under the bonnet).

Wash the headlamps.

Check the oil (see below).

Dipstick

Mark

Check the oil by removing the dipstick from the engine (ask the driver where it is). Wipe it on a rag, replace it, then remove it again. Look to see if the oil comes up to the mark on the stick. Tell the driver if it doesn't, wipe the dipstick and replace it.

3

Journey log

Before setting off you could make a journey log, like the one shown opposite, to record details of your journey. The picture below explains the instruments you're likely to find on the car dashboard to help fill in some of the details on your log. All cars vary, so ask the driver where the instruments are in your car.

Dashboard instruments

1 Speedometer – shows the car's speed, usually both in kilometers per hour (kph) and miles per hour (mph).

2 Odometer – shows how far the car has been driven since it was made.

3 Trip counter – shows how far the car has been on a particular journey. Ask the driver to set this before leaving.

4 Tachometer – tells the speed of the engine in thousands of revolutions per minute. This often looks like the speedometer, so ask the driver which is which as you don't need to use this one. Not all cars have them.

5 Petrol gauge – shows how much petrol is in the tank. They are usually marked so you can see if the tank is full, ¾ full, ½ full or empty. Ask the driver how much petrol the tank holds when full. You can then work out roughly how much petrol is in the tank. Or, if the driver fills up with petrol when the tank is empty, you can see how much has been put in by looking at the petrol pump.

Making the log

It is a good idea to make your journey log in a separate book. You can then make a new log for each journey and keep a record of everywhere you go. After a year you could work out how many towns you have passed through, how far you have travelled and so on. Make your log like this:

1 Draw lines to divide the pages up into three boxes; the top for when you set off, the middle for the journey, and the bottom for when you arrive.

2 Divide up the boxes as shown. For the middle section you will need to look at a map to see how many towns you expect to pass through, and to work out places of interest on the route.

3 Fill-in the details as you go.

| Amount of petrol in tank | 22 litres | | Odometer reading | 035355 | Departure time | 9.30 a.m. |
| Trip reading | | | | 00000 | Weather | Rain |

Towns passed through. (Tick when spotted)		Places of interest (Tick when spotted)	
CASTLETOWN	✓	BIGDROP CASTLE	✓
SPLASHRIVER FALLS	✓	OLD RUINS	✓
FALLOVER DOWNS	✓	NATURE PARK	✓
TIMBERFELLS	✓	GREENTOP FOREST	✓
STEAMVILLE	✓	OLD RAILWAY STATION	✓
NOTQUITA CITY	✓	AIRPORT	✓
ALMOSTHERE TOWN	✓	AUNTY FLO'S HOUSE	✓
GORILLATON	✓	NATURE PARK	✓

Distance Travelled	Time	Weather
5 km	9.40	Rain
25 Km	10.10	Rain
49 Km	10.40	Rain
73 Km	11.15	Still. Raining!
93 Km	11.40	Stopped raining!
105 Km	11.55	Cloudy
125 Km	12.15	Sunny – at last!
150 Km	12.30	Still Sunny!

Time of arrival	12.30 p.m.
Total journey time	3 hours
Odometer reading	035505
Trip reading	00150
Amount of petrol used	13 litres

Average petrol consumption (Divide distance travelled by amount of petrol used.) **11 Kms. per litre**

Average speed (Divide distance travelled by time taken.) **50 kph**

Treasure hunt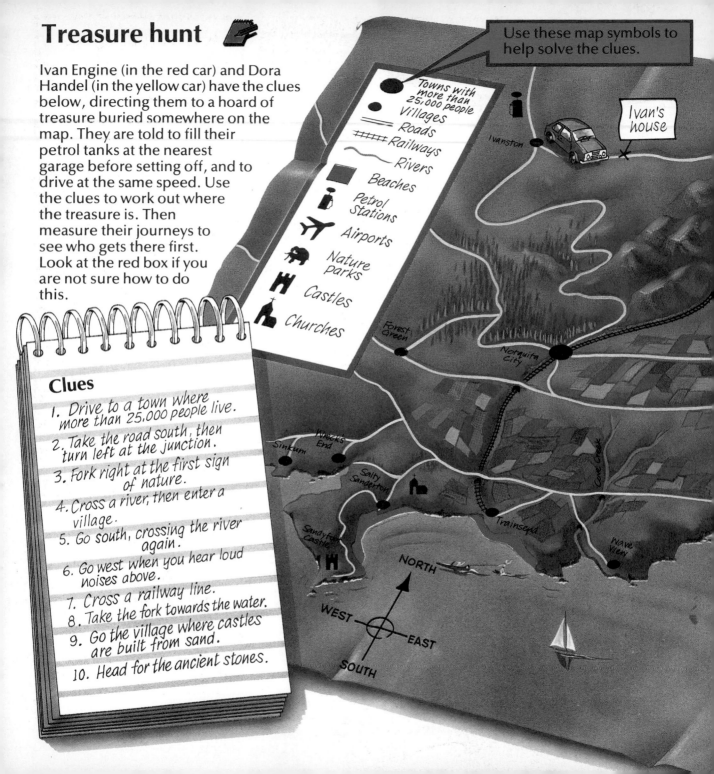

Ivan Engine (in the red car) and Dora Handel (in the yellow car) have the clues below, directing them to a hoard of treasure buried somewhere on the map. They are told to fill their petrol tanks at the nearest garage before setting off, and to drive at the same speed. Use the clues to work out where the treasure is. Then measure their journeys to see who gets there first. Look at the red box if you are not sure how to do this.

Use these map symbols to help solve the clues.

Towns with more than 25,000 people
Villages
Roads
Railways
Rivers
Beaches
Petrol Stations
Airports
Nature parks
Castles
Churches

Ivan's house

Ivanston

Forest Green

Norquita City

Cove Creek

Weaks End

Sinkum

Salty Sanderton

Sandyford Castle

Trainseyd

Wave View

NORTH
WEST
EAST
SOUTH

Clues

1. Drive to a town where more than 25,000 people live.
2. Take the road south, then turn left at the junction.
3. Fork right at the first sign of nature.
4. Cross a river, then enter a village.
5. Go south, crossing the river again.
6. Go west when you hear loud noises above.
7. Cross a railway line.
8. Take the fork towards the water.
9. Go the village where castles are built from sand.
10. Head for the ancient stones.

The scale shows how many km (or miles) there are to each cm (or inch) on the map.

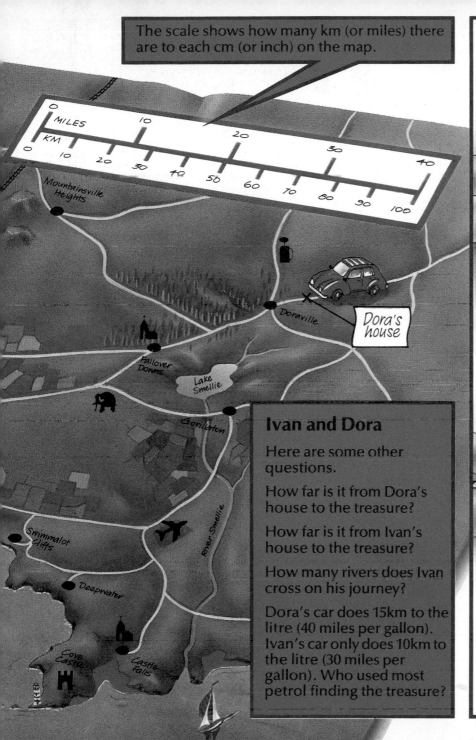

Measuring distances

The steps below show how to find out actual distances between two points on a map.

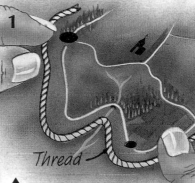

1

Thread

▲
Hold a piece of thread along the line of the road between the points you want to measure.

2

Ruler

▲
Hold the thread tight against the scale of the map or a ruler to measure the distance in cm or inches.

Actual distance = length of thread × number of km (or miles) in one cm (or inch).

Ivan and Dora

Here are some other questions.

How far is it from Dora's house to the treasure?

How far is it from Ivan's house to the treasure?

How many rivers does Ivan cross on his journey?

Dora's car does 15km to the litre (40 miles per gallon). Ivan's car only does 10km to the litre (30 miles per gallon). Who used most petrol finding the treasure?

7

Secret agent

James Pond, secret agent, is at a garage 150km (90 miles) from safety over the border in Venuzlulu. S.Q.U.A.S.H. agents are 50km (30 miles) behind, driving at 150kph (90mph). James buys a getaway car, but it has a slight fault. See if you can work out which car he buys to escape from the enemy in time. Hint: work out how long the agents take to get to the border, then how long each car would take.

This car is so rusty that its floor will drop out if driven faster than 150kph (90mph).

...jeep only has reverse gear, but goes backwards at 100kph(60mph).

Signpost

Tara Mack puts up seven of the warning signs on the right on the planet Auto, at the places shown by the numbered triangles. See if you can write a list of the signs she takes, in the order she puts them up. Match the letter beside the signs with the number in the triangles.

Tara Mack

A

B

C

D

E

F

G

H

1

2

3

The blue car does 50kph (30mph). Its radiator leaks, though, and after half an hour the engine overheats and stops.

The orange pick-up does 150kph (90mph), but needs new spark plugs every 15 minutes. These take 10 minutes to fit.

◄ The red sports car does 300kph (180mph), but its petrol tank leaks and is empty after 20 minutes.

How far?

This blue car takes three minutes at 30kph (20mph) to reach the top of the hill and three minutes at twice the speed to reach the bottom. How far has it travelled?

Did you know?

There are over 400 million cars in the world – a third in the USA. If every car were parked bumper to bumper, they would go round the equator 41 times.

You could see how many warning signs you can spot. Draw a picture of each one and then tick beside the picture every time you spot the sign. Score 5 points for spotting at least two of each sign.

Cops and robbers

Split into two teams – cops and robbers. The cops want to catch the robbers, but five oil drums block the way. The robbers can't escape because their tyres are all punctured (including the spare). Take turns to ask the other team questions, using those below, or ideas of your own. For each correct answer the cops remove an oil drum or the robbers mend a puncture. The cops make an arrest by removing all the oil drums, but the robbers escape by mending all the punctures.

Bus stop

Split into two teams and each take one side of the road. Count the number of people waiting at bus stops on your side. The first team to count to 100 wins.

Questions

Which city is the capital of Norway?

How long is a decade?

Where would you see the Mona Lisa?

Who said, "Elementary my dear Watson?"

Where do Maoris live?

What's big and red and eats rocks?

What's 7 x 9?

What's odd about the buses in Venice?

How long is a piece of string?

Keep your score on a piece of paper.

Legs

Split into two teams. Each team has to count the number of legs on one side of the road, including bench legs, dogs' legs, statue legs and so on. The winning team is the first to reach 100.

How many legs did the teams in the red car count? Score 5 points for the right answer.

Tunnel

Aver is 30km (20 miles) from Lanch by mountain road and 15km (10 miles) using the tunnel. It takes 10 minutes to queue for the tunnel. Which is the fastest route driving at 60kph (40mph).

Autogram

HONDA = Had on

RENAULT = Late run

Make a list of all the different car and truck names you can think of or spot out of the window. Then try unscrambling them to make new words like those above.

Who lives there?

Take turns to describe the owners of unusual houses seen on your journey. Imagine what they look like, their favourite food, the pets they keep and so on.

Aerials and exhaust pipes

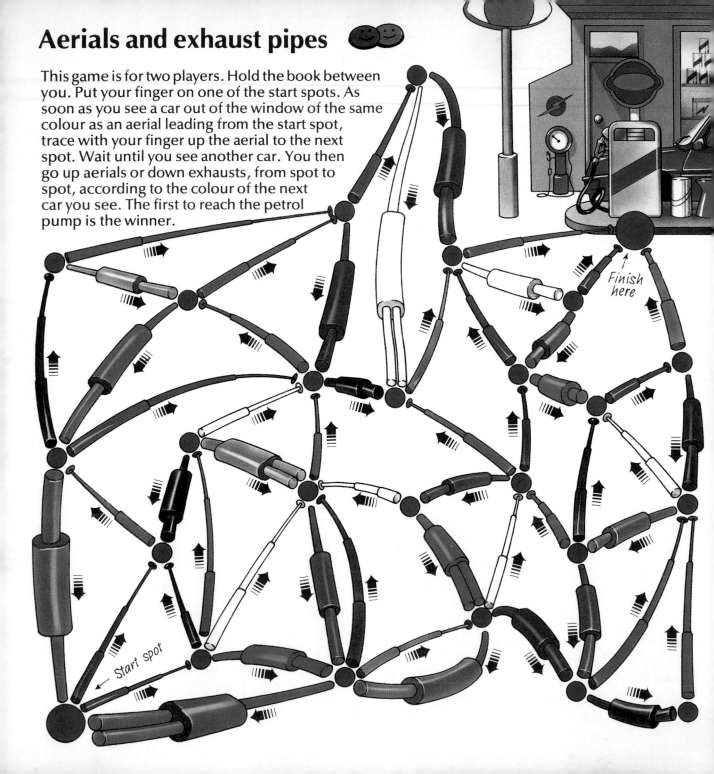

This game is for two players. Hold the book between you. Put your finger on one of the start spots. As soon as you see a car out of the window of the same colour as an aerial leading from the start spot, trace with your finger up the aerial to the next spot. Wait until you see another car. You then go up aerials or down exhausts, from spot to spot, according to the colour of the next car you see. The first to reach the petrol pump is the winner.

Finish here

Start spot

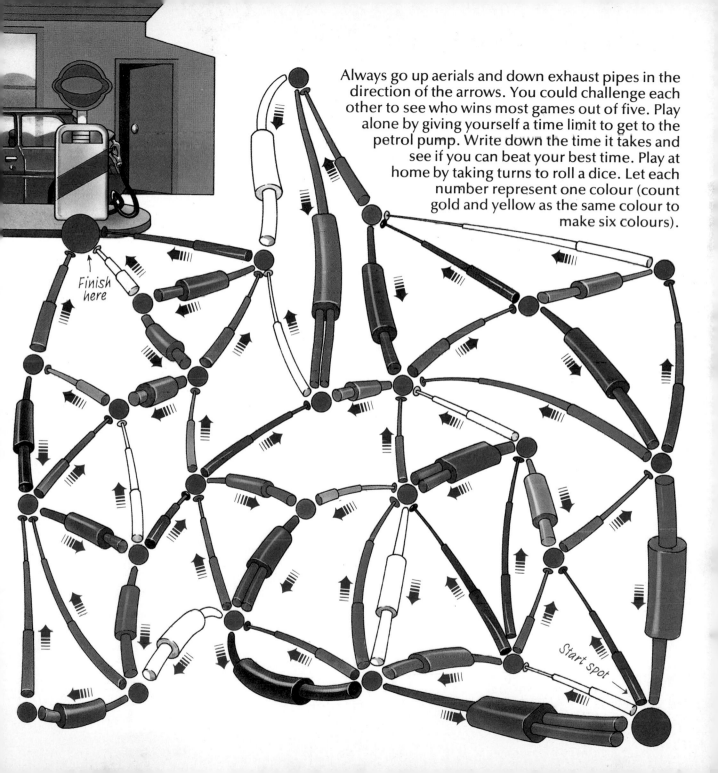

Always go up aerials and down exhaust pipes in the direction of the arrows. You could challenge each other to see who wins most games out of five. Play alone by giving yourself a time limit to get to the petrol pump. Write down the time it takes and see if you can beat your best time. Play at home by taking turns to roll a dice. Let each number represent one colour (count gold and yellow as the same colour to make six colours).

Finish here

Start spot

Fred's car

Fred's car uses all the parts below after the distances shown. He pays for them in car keys where he lives (on the planet Auto). See if you can work out Fred's bill, in car keys, after driving 100,000km (60,000 miles).

Two fan belts every 20,000km (12,000 miles). Price: two keys each.

Six spark plugs every 5,000km (3,000 miles). Price: 5 keys each.

One air filter every 10,000km (6,000 miles). Price: 1 key each.

One can of oil every 5,000km (3,000 miles). Price: 10 keys a can.

Three tyres every 10,000km (6,000 miles). Price: 20 keys each.

Navigator

Mark Skidd decided to visit his Aunty on the other side of town. Before setting off he made a chart like the one below. In each column he wrote a guess of how many times he would go round a roundabout, turn left, right or go through traffic lights. He then kept a count of how often he actually made these movements on the journey.

Mark drove to his Aunty's by the shortest route. How many times did he guess his movements correctly?

Make a chart like Mark's for your own journey and score five points for each correct guess you make.

Hint: Look at a map before leaving to work out the movements you might make.

MOVEMENTS	ROUND-ABOUTS	LEFT TURNS	RIGHT TURNS	TRAFFIC LIGHTS
GUESSES	2	2	9	4
ACTUAL MOVEMENTS	?	?	?	?

Pink toads

What do you eat for breakfast?

Take turns to ask each other silly questions. The answer must always be, "Pink toads". You're out if you laugh when you answer. The winner is the last person left.

Quick games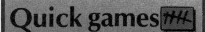

1 Everyone (except the driver) shuts their eyes and listens to the car. After a while, the driver asks what the car's speed is. The nearest answer scores 5 points.

2 Take turns to guess the colour of the next car to come round a bend. Score 1 point if you guess correctly.

3 Play "car spy" (like "I spy"). Start with, "I spy with my little eye, a car beginning with . . . " Use the first letter of car names you see.

Did you know?

The first car radio in the world was fitted to a Ford Model T in 1922 by a driver in Chicago, USA.

Missing parts

A mechanic re-built these old cars, but forgot at least 16 things from the one on the right.

Score one point for each missing part you find.

Destination

This game is for two players, starting at opposite ends of the road. The winner is the first to get to the other end. Make the counters shown below, before leaving home, and use Blu-tack* to stick them to the book.

Take turns to spot things from the chart opposite to move your counter along the road. You must move the number of squares shown beside each thing. If you land on a white square, your next move must be in the direction shown by the arrow.

Go straight through tunnels to get to the other side of the page.

How to make counters

Paper

For each counter, trace this picture on paper and glue it to thin card.

Cut round here

Card

Scissors

Colour the car, then cut as shown.

Blu-tack

Bend here

Bend the counter along the dotted line so it stands up. Then stick a piece of Blu-tack* underneath.

Player 1 starts here

*Blu-tack is the trade name for a sticky putty used to hang posters on the wall.

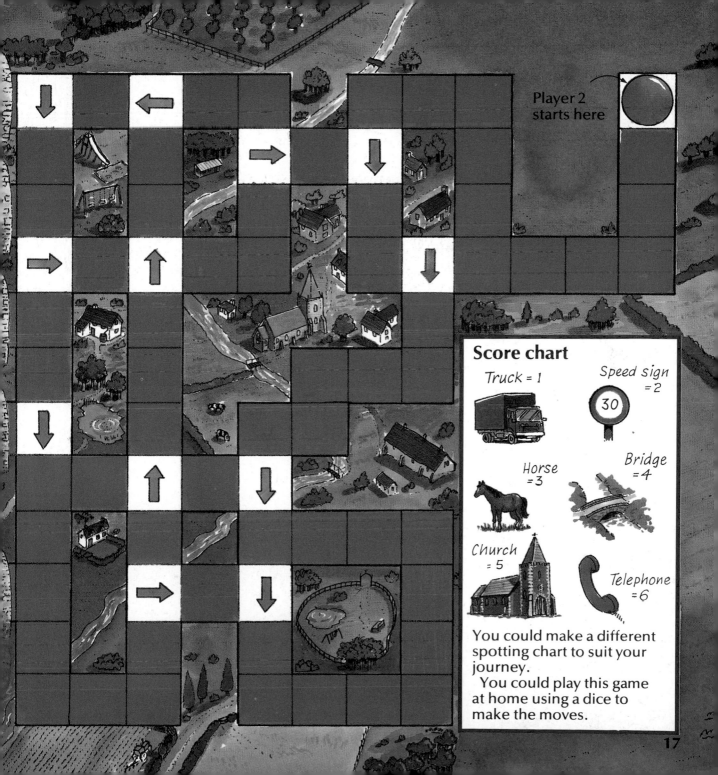

Player 2
starts here

Score chart

Truck = 1

Speed sign = 2

Horse = 3

Bridge = 4

Church = 5

Telephone = 6

You could make a different spotting chart to suit your journey.

You could play this game at home using a dice to make the moves.

17

Zoo

The idea of this game is to be first to collect 20 "animals" for a zoo. First write down a list of animals to be captured by spotting certain things out of the window. The notepad on the right gives some ideas – a park bench could count as an elephant, a policeman as a tiger and so on. Everyone has to use the same list and remember what's on it.

You capture an "animal" by being first to spot it and call out its name. It escapes if you call it by the wrong name, but can be captured by someone else. The first person to fill their zoo scores 10 points.

Escape

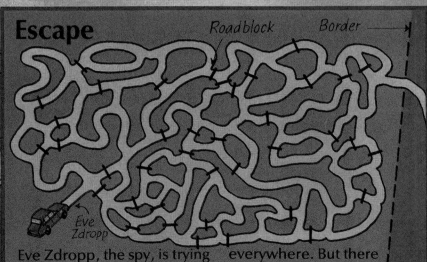

Roadblock   Border

Eve Zdropp

Eve Zdropp, the spy, is trying to escape from the police. Unfortunately, they seem to have set-up road blocks everywhere. But there is one route to safety across the border – can you find it?

Did you know?

Nearly 20 million Volkswagen Beetles have been produced. 26,000 football pitches would be needed to park them all at once.

Number cruncher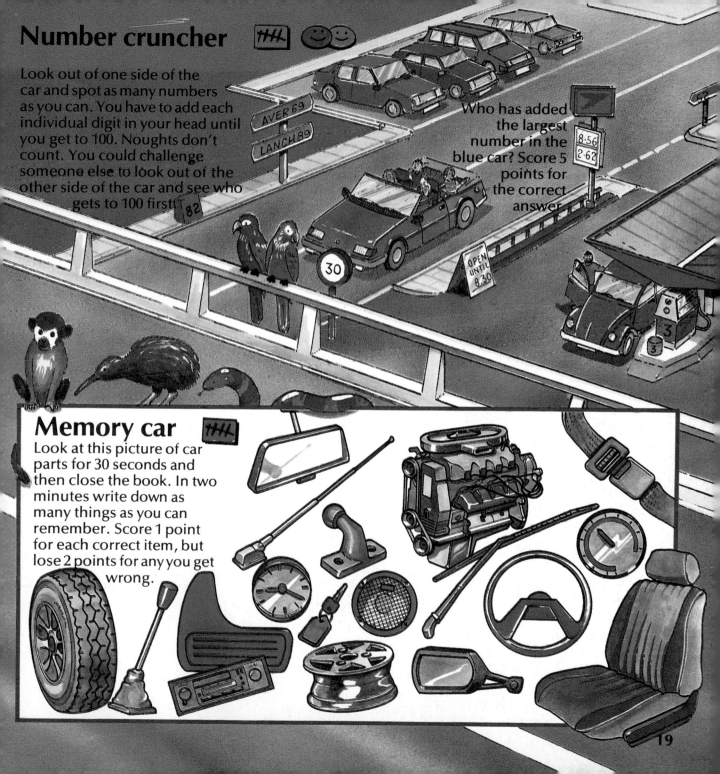

Look out of one side of the car and spot as many numbers as you can. You have to add each individual digit in your head until you get to 100. Noughts don't count. You could challenge someone else to look out of the other side of the car and see who gets to 100 first.

AVER 69
LANCH 89
82

Who has added the largest number in the blue car? Score 5 points for the correct answer.

8·56
2·62

30

OPEN UNTIL 8.30

3
3

Memory car

Look at this picture of car parts for 30 seconds and then close the book. In two minutes write down as many things as you can remember. Score 1 point for each correct item, but lose 2 points for any you get wrong.

Word race

This game is for up to five players. Make counters as shown on page 16 – one for each driver. Choose one of the lanes at the start of the track and stick your counter to the blue square with Blu-tack.

Look for words on signs out of the car window. When you spot a word beginning with the letter on the diamond in front of you, move your counter forwards to the next blue section of your lane.

At the same time, you can (if you want to) move sideways in the new section across one of the orange diamonds, to put your counter in a different lane.

By doing this you will be able to block the path of another driver, as only one driver at a time is allowed on a blue square.

The winner is the first to get to the finish line.

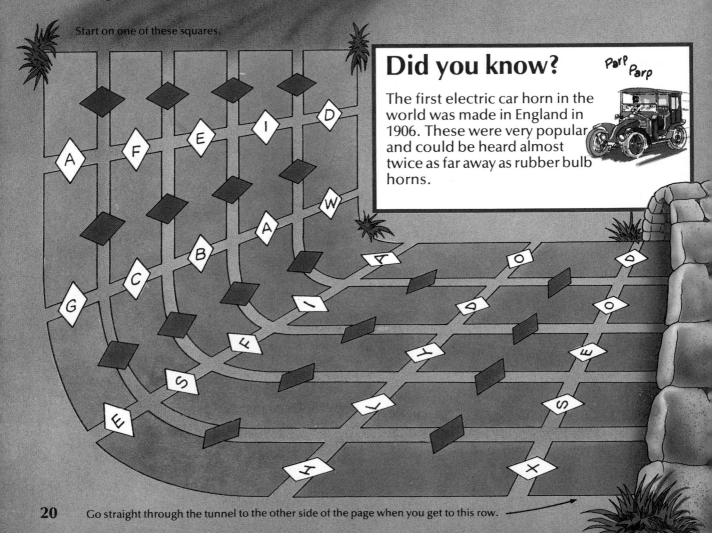

Start on one of these squares.

Did you know?

Parp Parp

The first electric car horn in the world was made in England in 1906. These were very popular and could be heard almost twice as far away as rubber bulb horns.

Go straight through the tunnel to the other side of the page when you get to this row.

Funny maps

Place a pad of paper on your knee and hold a blunt pencil over the paper without it touching. As you go over bumps, the pencil will touch the paper and draw a funny map. You could colour in your map when you stop for a break.

Signpost

Everyone has to guess how long it will take to get from one signpost to the next. Write your guesses down and time how long it actually takes using a watch. The person with the nearest guess scores 1 point.

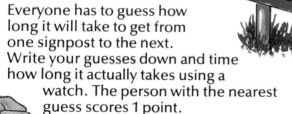

You could decide to do more than one lap of the race. Go back to the start line when you get to the end if you want to do this.

Collector's quest

Make a list of ten things to collect and bring home from an outing. Try to think of things likely to be found at your destination, but don't include anything too large to fit in the car. Score 5 points for each item you collect.

Look at this beach scene to see how many things you can spot from the list below. Score 1 point for every item you find.

Piece of seaweed
Seashell
Feather
Coin
Piece of string
Plastic bottle
Piece of driftwood
Beach ball
Ice-cream stick
Pebble with a hole through it

Speedy

| 0 | 10 | 20 | 30 | 40 | 50 | 60 | 70 | 80 | 90 | 100 |

For this game you need a copy of the speedometer above for each player. You then colour it in, 5 or 10kph (or mph) at a time, by being first to say "speedy" when you spot something from the charts on the right. The first to reach top speed is the winner.

Spotting these increases your speed by 5kph (or mph).

Blue trucks

Caravans

Bicycles

Taxis

Coaches

Spotting these increases your speed by 10kph (or mph).

Foreign number plates

Cats

Bridges

Rivers

Trains

Hungry alphabet

Take turns to say what you want for dinner, like the people in the red car below. The person who starts must choose something beginning with "A". The next person repeats what the first person said and then adds something beginning with "B", and so on until you get to "Z".

I'm so hungry I could eat an apple and a bean

I'm so hungry I could eat an apple and a bean and custard

I'm so hungry I could eat an apple

Did you know?

The world uses 2,320,000,000 litres (510,380,000 gallons) of petrol every day. This is enough for every car in the world to use 5.6 litres (1.2 gallons) a day.

Car thief

Hugh Snapper was taking photos of the moon from his bedroom window one night, when a thief stole his car, parked below. Hugh took a picture of the trail made by the escaping car's lights. Use the photo and map to tell the police which streets the thief took, and where he parked the car.

Hats off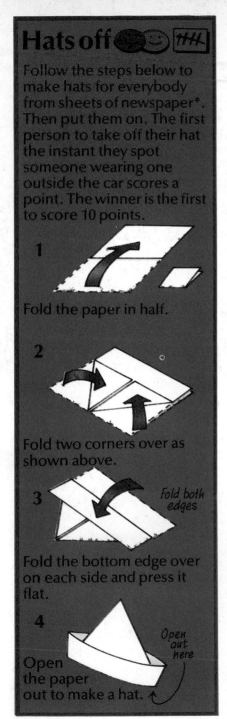

Follow the steps below to make hats for everybody from sheets of newspaper*. Then put them on. The first person to take off their hat the instant they spot someone wearing one outside the car scores a point. The winner is the first to score 10 points.

1

Fold the paper in half.

2

Fold two corners over as shown above.

3

Fold both edges

Fold the bottom edge over on each side and press it flat.

4

Open out here

Open the paper out to make a hat.

Delivery

Eva Packett has to deliver parcels to each of the ten houses in the picture above. See if you can work out her starting point, and the route she should take to avoid driving down any street more than once.

Polar puzzle

Imagine you've driven to the North Pole. In which direction should you go to get home?

Did you know?

It would take one constantly running petrol pump 397 years to dispense all the petrol used in the world in one day.

*You could use a large sheet of ordinary paper instead.

Street story

Take turns to make up a funny story using words spotted on street signs, in shop windows, on truck sides and so on.

Look at the picture above and see if you can continue this story:
"Yesterday I walked along Apple Street, met Albert the gorilla and then ate an ice-cream in a bird's nest. Later I . . ."

Insultabot

Choose one person to act as a "robot". Take turns to ask the robot questions about yourself beginning with the words, "Am I . . .?" The robot is allowed to insult you by replying according to the first thing it sees from the chart on the right. You can see how the game works in the picture.

Choose a new robot after an agreed distance. You could write your own list of things to spot with new insults.

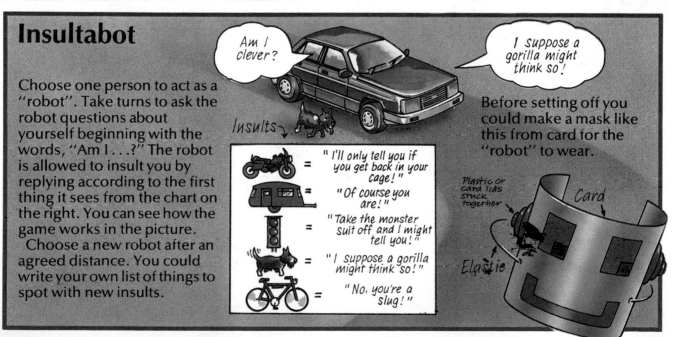

Am I clever?

I suppose a gorilla might think so!

Insults

= "I'll only tell you if you get back in your cage!"

= "Of course you are!"

= "Take the monster suit off and I might tell you!"

= "I suppose a gorilla might think so!"

= "No, you're a slug!"

Before setting off you could make a mask like this from card for the "robot" to wear.

Plastic or card has stuck together

Card

Elastic

Travel consequences

For this game you need a piece of paper for each player. Start by asking everyone to write a funny name at the top of the paper. Then fold the paper over, to conceal the name, like this:

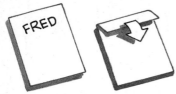

Pass your paper to the person sitting next to you, so they go round in a circle. Continue by writing things which fit the sequence of phrases shown on the right, folding the papers and passing them round each time.

Went to...

And met...

They said...

And decided to go to...

But, on the way...

So they decided to...

At the end, unfold the papers and read them out, using the words in the speech bubbles to make sentences for each section.

> FRED
> THE SOUTH POLE
> KING KONG
> FANCY MEETING YOU HERE
> A CINEMA
> THEIR CAR BROKE DOWN
> GO FISHING INSTEAD

Banana

One person goes to "sleep" by covering their ears and closing their eyes. Then everyone else picks one verb between them. Verbs are "doing" words, like run, jump, sleep, sit, sneeze and so on.

Get the person to "wake up" when the verb has been agreed. They then have to discover the chosen word by asking up to ten questions, changing the verb in the question to, "Banana". For example, they could ask, "Do you banana in the car?", or, "Am I bananaring right now?".

The sleepy person scores 5 points if they guess the verb from 10 or less questions. Then change players.

Suitcase

Here are some things you might like to take on holiday. Each choose ten things from the picture and write a list of your choices. Draw a picture beside each item, like this:

Teddy bear
Car
Slippers
Beach ball
Bat
Gloves
Socks
Cards
Towel
Hat

To be allowed your choice you have to spot things beginning with the same letter (or letters if the item is two words) and of the same colour. For example, to take a teddy bear you could spot something like a brown truck badge.

Call, "Suitcase" when you spot something and tell everyone what it is so they can check the spelling and colour. Then tick the item on your list.

The winner is the first person to tick everything on their list and scores 5 points.

Duck and jump

Everyone has five "lives". Lift your feet when going over bridges and duck when going under them. You lose a life if you forget. The last person "alive" wins.

East and west

Sid Speedy's car was facing west. After driving for five minutes Sid found that he'd actually gone east. How did this happen?

Where am I?

Play this game on a route you know well. Cover your eyes until the driver calls, "Ready". Then guess where you are. The person with the nearest guess wins.

Road builder

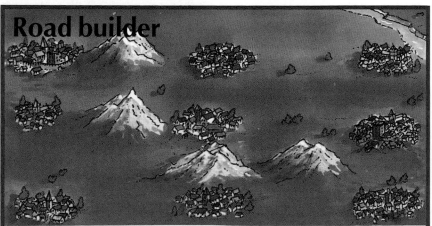

Nine villages in the mountains were cut off from each other until a road builder linked them together. He was told to build four straight stretches of road, but was not allowed to go over or through any mountain. See if you can draw a picture of the route he worked out.

Quick games 😊😊

1 Each write down something to spot. Call, "Pairs" each time you see a pair of your things. The winner is the first to spot ten pairs.

2 Guess how many traffic lights out of ten you will be able to go through without having to stop. The winner is the person with the nearest guess.

Spy bingo

Before setting off make a bingo card like the one below for each person, with pictures of things to spot. Each card should have the same pictures, but in a different order. You could just write names of things in each square if you don't want to draw the pictures.

Tyre puzzle

Three large and three small tyres are lined up like this:

Move two together

Re-arrange them to make the pattern above in three moves. You are allowed to move any two adjacent tyres and can put them at either end of the row, or in a gap if you make space by moving some to either end. Use coins to help solve the puzzle.

1

One person acts as the "caller", looking out of the car window to spot things from the card. As they call things out, cross them off on your card.

2

The first person to get a horizontal or vertical line of crosses and shout out, "Spy bingo!" is the winner. You could carry on to see who comes second.

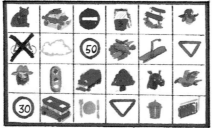

Did you know?

The first country in the world to introduce driving tests was France, first in Paris in 1893 and then in the rest of the country in 1899.

Answers

Page 6
Treasure hunt

The buried treasure was found first by Dora, at Sandyfoot Castle.

It is 515km (320 miles) from Dora's house to the treasure.

It is 550km (341 miles) from Ivan's house to the treasure.

Ivan crosses two rivers on his journey (he crosses the River Smellie twice).

Ivan uses most petrol finding the treasure (55 litres/12 gallons).

Page 8
Secret Agent

James Pond should buy the car with the rusty floor. This will get him over the border with 20 minutes to spare.

Signpost

Here is the order in which Tara Mack and her gang put up the road signs.

B1 C2 E3 H4 I5 K6 N7

Page 9
How far?

The blue car travels 4½km (3 miles) altogether.

Page 10
Cops and robbers

Here are the answers to the quiz:

Oslo is the capital city of Norway.

A decade is 10 years.

The Mona Lisa is in the Louvre, Paris.

Sherlock Holmes said, "Elementary my dear Watson".

Maoris come from New Zealand.

Big red rock eaters are big and red and eat rocks.

$7 \times 9 = 63$

The buses in Venice are boats.

A piece of string can be as long as you like.

Page 11
Legs

There are 66 legs in the picture.

Page 11 (continued)
Tunnel

The route through the tunnel is fastest – five minutes faster than by mountain road.

Page 14
Fred's car

Fred's bill comes to 1,530 keys.

Navigator

Mark made two correct guesses of his movements on the way to his Aunty's house. Here is the route he took.

Page 15
Missing parts

The parts missing from the car on the right are circled in the picture below.

Page 18
Escape

Here is the route Eve Zdropp uses to escape from the police.

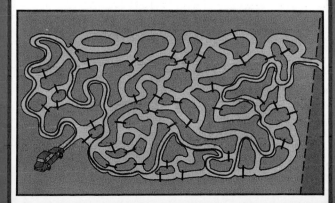

Page 19
Number cruncher

The team on the left of the car (nearest the garage) have the largest number.

Page 23
Car thief

Here is the route the thief took. He stopped in Short Acre.

Page 24
Delivery

This is the route Eva Packett takes to deliver her parcels.

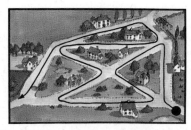

Polar puzzle

You would have to go south to get home as this is the only direction you can go from the North Pole.

Page 28
East and west

Sid went east because the car was in reverse gear.

Road builder

This is how the road builder linked the villages with only four stretches of road.

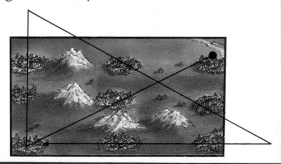

Page 29
Tyre puzzle

Here is the sequence of moves to rearrange the tyres.

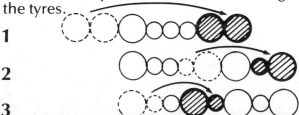

1

2

3

The publishers would like to thank Books at Home for ideas contributed to this book.

PART TWO

AIR TRAVEL GAMES

Moira Butterfield

Edited by Tony Potter

**Designed by Kim Blundell
and Nerissa Davies**

**Illustrated by Kim Blundell,
Chris Lyon and Guy Smith**

Contents

About this book

There are lots of games, puzzles and activities in this book to play on air journeys or at home. Some can be played on your own, others in teams.

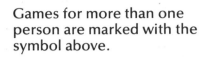

Games for more than one person are marked with the symbol above.

Long games are marked with this clock symbol. Save these until you have plenty of time to play them.

Fly with Mugsair

Below are the crew and passengers of Mugsair Airlines flight 321. They are about to fly from Fogsville airport to a holiday resort called Costa Fortune. You will meet them again on their journey in some of the games and puzzles in this book.

Crews are made up of cabin attendants and flight crew, such as the Captain, First Officer and Engineer. On a long flight you could ask an attendant if you can meet the Captain. On a short journey the flight crew will probably be too busy to meet passengers.

CREW

Flight attendant Ivor Tray
Flight Engineer Wil Itfly
James Pond
Rick Ord
1st. Officer Lou Smyway
Flight attendant Donna Panic
Captain Slog

PASSENGERS

Birdman Jack
Mr D. Racula
Lady Lollybags
Lotta Trouble
Ian Trouble
Peter Perfect
Mrs Flight
Mrs Bagsfull & baby

Captain's hat

Lots of the puzzles in this book
are marked with a picture of a
Captain's hat like the one
above. Each hat has a number marked on it. If
you answer one of these puzzles correctly
you can score the points shown on the hat.
Keep a note of your scores and add them up
when you have done all the Captain's hat
puzzles in the book.

You could get up to 55 points. If you score
over 40 points you qualify as an:

AIR TRAVEL GAMES CAPTAIN

Things you can take

You need to take the things below to be
able to play some of the games in this
book. It is a good idea to pack them in
one small bag.

If you would like to keep a record of
your air flight there is a Captain's log to
make on page 61   You need to get this
ready before you start your journey.

Pencils or crayons   Drawing pad

Tear-off
notepad
for
scoring.

Dice or scorer

How to make a scorer

If you don't have a dice
you can make a scorer to use
instead. You need a piece
of stiff plain paper, some
tracing paper, a pair of
scissors, a pencil and a used
match or something similar.

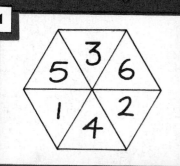

1

Trace the shape and lines
above onto tracing paper, as
carefully as you can.

2 Stiff paper → Tracing paper

Put the tracing paper on top of
the stiff paper, with the pencil
marks face-downwards. Draw
over them with a pencil to
transfer the scorer shape to the
stiff paper.

3 Draw over these lines to stop
them smudging.

Carefully cut out the shape and
mark one side with the
numbers as shown in step 1.

4

Push the match through the
middle of the shape as
shown above. You might
find this easier to do if you
first make a small hole with a
scissor point.

5 A score of four.

Spin the scorer round on a
table, like a top. You score
the number shown on the
edge which comes to rest.

Answers to all the puzzles in this book are on pages 62-64

Camera clues

The Mugsair passengers are queuing to board their plane. A security guard is watching them on a video screen, but his camera is faulty and it has changed the picture. See if you can spot at least ten differences between the camera picture and the real scene.

VIDEO SCREEN

Let us out!

The Mugsair crew and flight attendants have accidentally been locked in the crew rest lounge. The key is in the wrong side of the door. See if you can work out how they get the key, using only the objects in the room.

The key is on the wrong side of this door.

Flight Engineer

1st Officer

Captain

Whose jacket?

Airline flight crews have stripes on their jacket sleeves to show what job they do. The different stripes are shown below. The three members of the Mugsair flight crew locked in the lounge on the left have put on the wrong jackets. See if you can work out who's wearing whose.

Captain	Senior First Officer

First Officer	Flight Engineer

Queuing quickies

Here are some quick games to try while queuing or waiting at the airport.

⭐ See how many direction signs you can spot to different parts of the airport. You could challenge someone else to see who can make the longest list.

⭐ See how many different jobs you can spot people doing at the airport. There is often a different kind of uniform for each kind of job. You could challenge a friend to see who spots the most.

⭐ Airport departure boards show the town or city, but not the country, where departing aeroplanes are flying to. Look at a departure board and see how many places you recognise. See if you can guess from the cities shown on the board below which countries the planes are going to visit.

Flight	Destination
323	Venice
297	Athens
345	Cairo
595	Moscow

Smuggler search

The escaped smuggler Hans Cuffed is shown below on a wanted poster.

Dick Lare, the Fogsville Customs Officer, has stopped four passengers. Their passport photos are on the right. One of them is Hans Cuffed in disguise, using a false name. Who do you think Dick should arrest as the smuggler?

Honor Plane

Abe Oveground

Ian Flightmovie

Ed Intheclouds

Dick Lare

In disguise

See how many ways you can disguise yourself by copying your passport photo* several times in a drawing pad, then adding different disguises to each drawing. There are some examples of disguises below.

Passport pieces

Some of the picture parts on the right are from Lady Lollybag's passport photo below. See if you can work out which ones don't fit.

Lady Lollybags

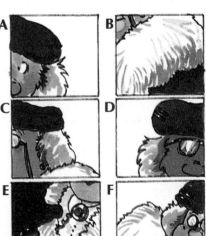

A B C D E F

*You could use an ordinary photo if you don't have a passport.

Anything to declare?

Air passengers arriving from abroad have to pay a tax, called "duty", for bringing some goods into the country. The Fogsville Customs Officers fine people if they find out that they have the goods but have not admitted it. In this game for three or more players everyone has a go at being a Customs Officer. Duty is paid in splots at Fogsville.

A splot

Things you need

Before you start you need to make ten "goods tickets" by copying the pictures and words on the right on to small pieces of paper. Put all the finished tickets into a bag. Each ticket shows an item and an amount of duty.

Goods tickets for you to make.

Ticket bag

Pair of earrings 2 splots duty
Bottle of whiskey 3 splots duty
Perfume 4 splots duty
Radio 5 splots duty
Watch 6 splots duty
Camera 8 splots duty
Diamond Ring 12 splots duty
Fur coat 13 splots duty
Necklace 15 splots duty
Diamond tiara 20 splots duty

How to play

1 One player starts off as the Customs Officer, the others as passengers. One passenger starts by picking out three goods tickets from the bag with their eyes closed.

2 Add up the ticket duty, and tell the Officer how much you owe. If your duty adds up to more than 25 splots, pretend you have less, like the player below.

I OWE 15 SPLOTS!

His duty adds up to 30 splots really.

3 The Officer can demand to see the tickets you picked out if he thinks you are fibbing about your total. If you have fibbed, the Customs Officer scores ten points.

Good Challenge. Score 10 Points

4 The Officer loses five points if his challenge is wrong. He must keep a note of how many points he scores. After your go put the tickets back in the bag for the next player.

Wrong Challenge. Lose 5 Points

5 Each passenger gets two turns at picking out tickets in a round. Choose a new Customs Officer from among the players after each round, until everyone has had a go.

6 The winner is the player who scores most points during their turn as Customs Officer. You could end up with less than zero if you make too many wrong challenges.

Potty's planes

Here are five aircraft built by Mugsair's mad inventor, Professor Potty. Which is the odd one out?

Sneaky spies

Top secret agent James Pond is one of the Mugsair passengers. He wants to get on the flight to Costa Fortune without being spotted by any enemy spies. Which way should he go through Fogsville airport to get to the plane without meeting any of them?

A spy looks like this

Entrance

James Pond

Air badges

Airline companies have their own badges. Look at the three pairs below to see if you can work out which of those in the box on the right makes up the fourth pair.

Aer Lingus (Ireland)	Air Canada
Pan Am (USA)	TWA (USA)

Qantas (Australia)	Icelandair
Lufthansa (W. Germany)	?

Gulf Air (Gulf States)

Swissair

Olympic (Greece)

Did you know?

The King Khalid International airport in Saudi Arabia is the largest in the world. It covers 221 sq.km (86 sq. miles), the size of 27,532 international football pitches. It also has the world's largest control tower.

Spy catching

Five enemy spies follow James Pond onto the Mugsair flight. They are all hiding on the following pages in this book. See if you can spot all of them as you go through.

Who is it?

Birdman Jack is on the Mugsair trip because he is going to spend a holiday with a relative in Costa Fortune: his mother's sister's father's wife. Who is he going to stay with?

Spot the planes

Lotta Trouble, Ian Trouble and Peter Perfect are plane spotting at Fogsville Airport, shown below. They have each made a list of the planes they can see, but only one is correct. Use the spotting guide on the right to work out which is the correct list.

Lotta
Boeing 747
DC9
DC10
Airbus

Ian
DC9
Boeing 747
Boeing 727
DC10

Peter
DC9
Airbus
Boeing 727
Boeing 747

Spotting guide

This spotting guide shows five popular planes, with some suggestions on things to look for to identify each aircraft. Four of them are parked at Fogsville airport below. You could use this guide to spot planes at your own airport.

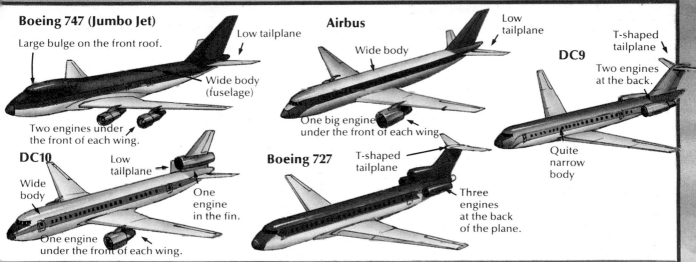

Boeing 747 (Jumbo Jet)

Large bulge on the front roof.

Low tailplane

Wide body (fuselage)

Two engines under the front of each wing.

Airbus

Wide body

Low tailplane

One big engine under the front of each wing.

DC9

T-shaped tailplane

Two engines at the back.

Quite narrow body

DC10

Low tailplane

Wide body

One engine in the fin.

One engine under the front of each wing.

Boeing 727

T-shaped tailplane

Three engines at the back of the plane.

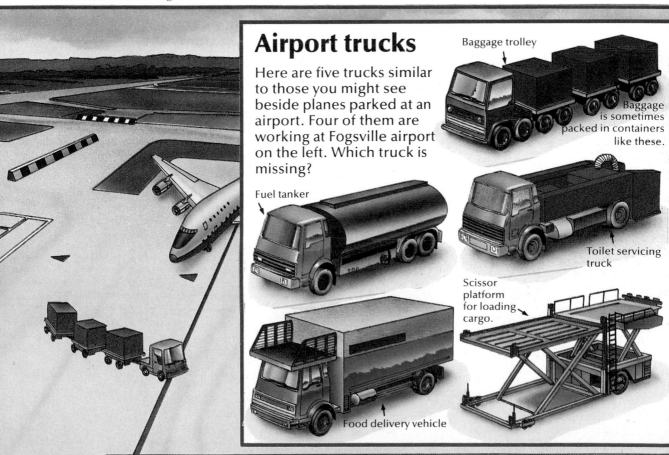

Airport trucks

Here are five trucks similar to those you might see beside planes parked at an airport. Four of them are working at Fogsville airport on the left. Which truck is missing?

Baggage trolley

Baggage is sometimes packed in containers like these.

Fuel tanker

Toilet servicing truck

Scissor platform for loading cargo.

Food delivery vehicle

Seating plan

Six Mugsair passengers are about to sit in a block of seats. See if you can work out who sits in which seat from the clues below.

James Pond sits behind Lady Lollybags.

Lady Lollybags sits by a window.

Rick Ord sits two seats along from James Pond

Lotta Trouble sits between two people.

Peter Perfect sits next to Lady Lollybags.

Mrs Bagsfull sits in the remaining seat.

A parking problem

Three differently coloured planes are on the wrong runways at Fogsville. Work out the best way to move them along the connecting paths (called taxiways) to their own runways, without allowing them to meet or park on the same runway together.

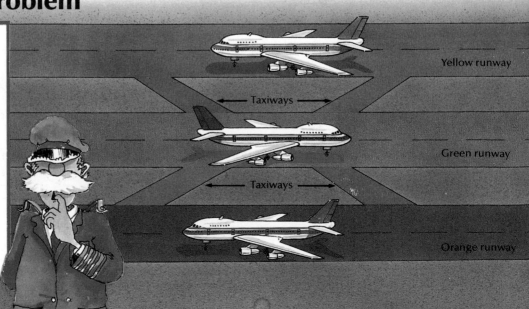

Truck mechanic

Hans Greasy, the Mugsair mechanic, has one hour to mend one of the trucks below. It takes him ten minutes to get some spark plugs from the store, and five minutes to find a spanner to fit wheel nuts. Which truck has he got time to mend?

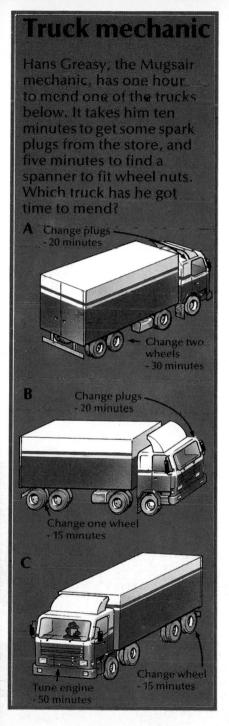

A Change plugs – 20 minutes

Change two wheels – 30 minutes

B Change plugs – 20 minutes

Change one wheel – 15 minutes

C Tune engine – 50 minutes

Change wheel – 15 minutes

The take-off race

This is a race to see who can load all the cargo onto their plane first and then take-off.

Take turns to throw a dice or spin a scorer. Look at the boxes below to see what cargo you can load for each number you score.

You have to throw some numbers more than once to finish the game.

You need to get two luggage containers, three cargo containers and so on.

Once you have loaded all the items shown in the boxes you must throw a six to take-off. The player who takes off first wins the game. It is a good idea to keep a list of items as you load them, as shown below.

MRS BAGSFULL'S LIST
Film 1
Luggage 1
Cargo 11
Fuel 1
Food 11

In-flight film
Collect 1 of these.

Luggage box
Collect 2 of these.

Cargo container
Collect 3 of these.

Fuel load
Collect 4 of these.

Food tray
Collect 5 of these.

Throw a **6** to take-off

THE GREAT AIR QUIZ

There are three possible answers to each question in this quiz. Write down the question number, then the letter of the answer you think is correct. If you don't know the right answer try making a good guess. You can check to see how many you got right by looking at page 63. You could also try this quiz with a group of friends. Read out the questions and keep a note of who answers correctly. The person with the highest score is the winner.

1 Who was Orville Wright?

a The tallest ever pilot.
b The pilot of the first plane.
c The first world baggage-handling champion.

2 Who was Louis Bleriot?

a The first ever flight attendant.
b A famous airline chef.
c The first person to fly across the English Channel.

3 What is a Zeppelin?

a An airship.
b A German sausage sandwich invented by Louis Bleriot.
c The round bit in a plane engine.

4 What is an aileron?

a An air travel sickness pill.
b The square bit in a plane engine.
c An aircraft wing flap.

5 What is an airbridge?

a A game of cards.
b A tightrope between two aeroplanes.
c A passage which links a plane to an airport terminal.

6 What is a biplane?

a A stripy aeroplane.
b An aeroplane with double wings.
c A computerized aeroplane.

7 Where is Orly airport?

a Fogsville.
b The Bahamas.
c Paris.

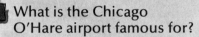

8 What is the Chicago O'Hare airport famous for?

a It sells the biggest hamburgers in the world.
b It is the busiest airport in the world.
c It was built in 1895.

9 What do aircraft builders use a wind tunnel for?

a Working out a plane's shape.
b Cleaning a plane.
c Drying their hair.

10 When was the first ever aeroplane flight?

a 1903
b 1744
c 1960

Now check your answers.

Air alphabet

Pilots use the "phonetic alphabet" to transmit clearly initial letters over the radio. They replace the initials with special words. Flight AS23 becomes "Alpha Sierra two three", for instance. The games on this page use the phonetic alphabet below.

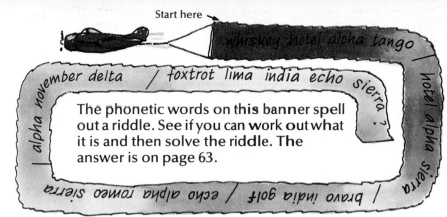

Start here

whiskey hotel alpha tango
alpha november delta / foxtrot lima india echo sierra
hotel alpha sierra
bravo india golf / echo alpha romeo sierra ?

The phonetic words on this banner spell out a riddle. See if you can work out what it is and then solve the riddle. The answer is on page 63.

A	Alpha	N	November
B	Bravo	O	Oscar
C	Charlie	P	Papa
D	Delta	Q	Quebec
E	Echo	R	Romeo
F	Foxtrot	S	Sierra
G	Gulf	T	Tango
H	Hotel	U	Uniform
I	India	V	Victor
J	Juliet	W	Whiskey
K	Kilo	X	X-ray
L	Lima	Y	Yankee
M	Mike	Z	Zebra

Did you know?

When you take off in a plane you get a popping feeling in your ears, because the pressure of the air around you goes down as you leave the ground. To get back to normal suck a boiled sweet, yawn or swallow.

Air story

There is one word from the phonetic alphabet missing in the story below. Which is it?

It was November in the Sierra. The Hotel Lima was fully booked. During the day many people played golf, and at night the echo of the foxtrot floated up from the dance floor into the air.

Papa Alpha , the head waiter, wore a smart red uniform. One night he organized a fancy dress competition. Mike, from Quebec, went as Romeo, and his wife went as Juliet. Charlie Delta went as a doctor.

But he drank too much whiskey, fell over doing the Tango, and had to go for an x-ray. Oscar from India was the victor, for his zebra outfit. Bravo! he won a kilo of chocolates.

Air race

This air race is for two players. The winner is the first person to get their plane from Fogsville to Cloudsville airport. You need a dice or a scorer (see page 35) and two counters to use as planes. Make one each by writing your name on a small slip of paper. Spread the book out on a flat surface to play.

How to play

1 Park your counter on one of the start squares. Take turns to throw the dice or spin the scorer. Move your plane the number of squares thrown.

2 You must start by flying along the route leading from your start square. Then obey the instructions on the squares you land on.

3 When both planes are on the same route they can overtake each other, but they cannot land on the same square.

4 If you throw a number which would land on the same square as another plane, stay where you are until your next go.

5 You must land on the same colour runway as you started, so you might need to change lanes at the end.

FOGSVILLE
DEPARTURE
RUNWAYS

START HERE.

DELAYED TAKE-OFF. MISS A GO.

PICK UP SPEED. GO FORWARD 2.

DIVERTED. CHANGE ROUTE.

START HERE.

DELAYED TAKE-OFF. MISS A GO.

PICK UP SPEED. GO FORWARD 2.

DIVERTED. CHANGE ROUTE.

48

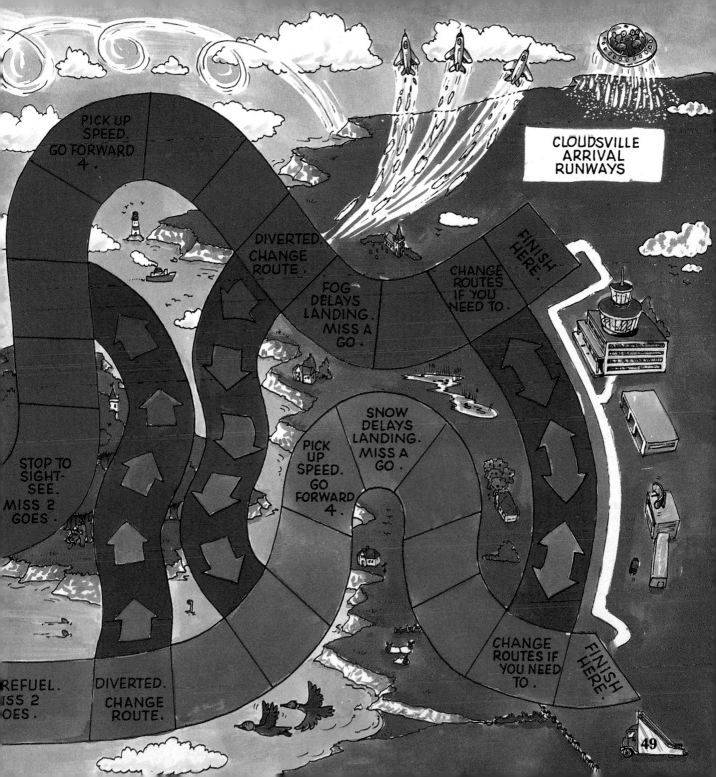

Time changes

The world is divided-up into 24 time zones. If you cross a time zone in an aeroplane you need to move your watch backwards or forwards, depending on the direction you are going in. When it is 1 o'clock in one zone, it is 2 o'clock in the zone to the east of it, and 12 o'clock in the zone to the west of it. See if you can work out the time puzzle on the right.

At 12 o'clock midday it is lunchtime in Fogsville.

Meanwhile, in Suntown people are shopping at 3 pm.

But in Snow City people are waking up at 8 am.

All the towns are marked on this map. Which is which?

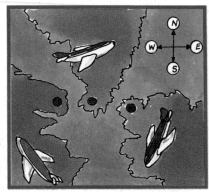

Alphabet row

Try playing this game on board a plane or waiting at an airport. For each passenger you see make up an imaginary name, a job and a place to live, using one letter of the alphabet, beginning at A.

For instance, you could start with Angus Addlebrain, an alligator catcher from Australia and move on to Brenda Boxhead, a brain surgeon from Birmingham, and so on through the alphabet to Z.

Make up the names quietly, so that you don't upset anyone.

" You could include imaginary names, jobs and homes for yourself and your companions in your list ! "

Flying fashion

These three flight attendants have got their uniforms all muddled up. See if you can work out who should be wearing what.

Jim

Bert

Mabel

Did you know?

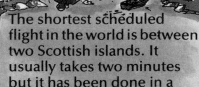

The shortest scheduled flight in the world is between two Scottish islands. It usually takes two minutes but it has been done in a record 58 seconds.

Fill the food tray

The idea of this game is for you to be a super-efficient flight attendant and collect as many things as you can to fill an airline food tray.

How to play

1 Use a small coin as your counter, or write your name on a small piece of paper.

2 Put your counter at the start and throw a dice or spin a scorer.

3 Move your counter along the row the number of spaces thrown. When you get to the end of a row follow the arrow to move down to the next one.

4 If you land on a space with an object on it, you can collect it for your tray. Make a note of what you collect.

5 If you land on a space which says you can go up or down, you can move to a different row and try to collect any items you have missed.

6 If you get to the end without collecting all the items, try again (start scoring again from the beginning). You could play with a friend to see who collects all the items first.

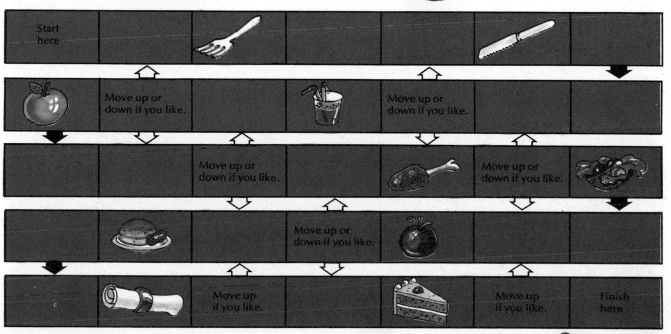

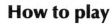

51

On autopilot

Lou Smyway, Mugsair First Officer, has switched on the autopilot (a machine that flies an aircraft) to guide the Mugsair plane from Fogsville to Costa Fortune. He has programmed the autopilot for a journey including six turns. See if you can work out the route it takes on the map shown on the right.

Fogsville

Costa Fortune

Fancy meeting you

A plane takes off from Fogsville airport on its way to Costa Fortune, 800 km away. Its speed is 350 km per hour. An hour later a plane takes off from Costa Fortune on its way to Fogsville, going at a speed of 400 km per hour.

As the planes pass each other which plane is nearest to Costa Fortune?

Did you know?

The longest human-powered flight was made in 1979 by a man who pedalled his specially designed craft for two hours and forty-nine minutes between Britain and France. His plane, called Gossamer Albatross, is shown above.

Music mimes

These four passengers are pretending to play the music on their in-flight headphones. See if you can guess which passengers are listening to which records.

RECORD LIST
a "Violin waltz"
b "Trumpet blues"
c "Rockin' drums"
d "Guitar Gertie"

Fit the food

See if you can work out which food tray belongs to which passenger from the clues below.

Ian Trouble wanted ice-cream. He didn't want a hot drink.

Birdman Jack wanted chips, but doesn't like sausages.

D. Racula didn't want ice-cream but did want sausages.

Mrs. Flight wanted a hot drink. She doesn't like chips.

The plane race

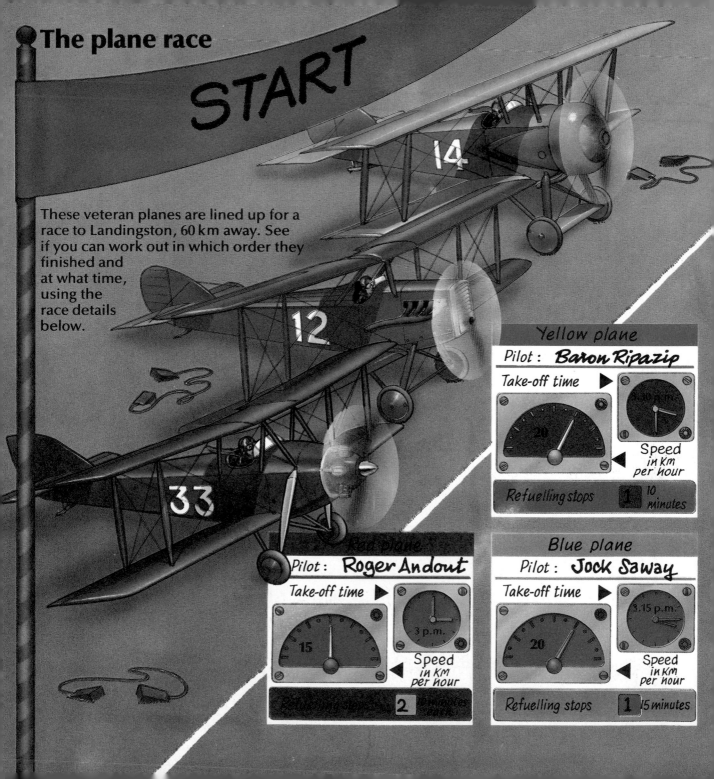

START

These veteran planes are lined up for a race to Landingston, 60 km away. See if you can work out in which order they finished and at what time, using the race details below.

Yellow plane

Pilot: **Baron Ripazip**

Take-off time ▶ 3.30 p.m.

20 ◀ Speed in km per hour

Refuelling stops | 1 | 10 minutes

Red plane

Pilot: **Roger Andout**

Take-off time ▶ 3 p.m.

15 ◀ Speed in km per hour

Refuelling stops | 2 | minutes each

Blue plane

Pilot: **Jock Saway**

Take-off time ▶ 3.15 p.m.

20 ◀ Speed in km per hour

Refuelling stops | 1 | 15 minutes

Air acrobatics

This airborne acrobatic team are doing a daring trick. See if you can work out how they made the second pyramid from the first pyramid by moving only three acrobats.

Mixed-up movie

The scenes in this in-flight film are all muddled up. See if you can work out in which order they should go.

Clear to land

Planes have to queue to land at busy airports by flying in circles at different levels. This is called "stacking". As soon as one plane lands, those above it fly down to the next level in the stack.

The idea of this game is to race with a friend to see who is first to land from one of the stacks below. Choose a stack each, then take it in turns to throw a dice or spin a scorer.

Start with your finger on the top level of your stack. Move down to the next level only when you throw the number shown on the dice beside it.

To play on your own, time how long it takes to move down a stack, then try to beat your best time.

START ON THIS LEVEL

START ON THIS LEVEL

THROW A SIX TO MOVE DOWN A LEVEL 6

THROW A FIVE TO MOVE DOWN A LEVEL 5

THROW A FOUR TO MOVE DOWN A LEVEL 4

THROW A THREE TO LAND 3

Marshalling maze

Marshals guide planes to parking bays at an airport. They use sticks or batons to make direction signals for pilots to follow. Some of these signals are shown on the right.

MOVE AHEAD   TURN RIGHT   TURN LEFT   STOP!

Follow the Mugsair marshal's signals in the box above to work out which parking bay the plane below is being directed to. Imagine you are the pilot looking out of the front of the aircraft.

Mystery number

3   6   11   18   ?

The numbers of these plane parking bays form a series. See if you can work out the number of the last bay.

Collect the cases

This is a race for two players, to see who can collect all their baggage first from one of the airport conveyor belts below. Each player needs a small coin to play.

Choose a conveyor belt each. The player on the left must collect all the numbered yellow cases. The player on the right must collect all the numbered red cases. Take turns to throw a dice or spin a scorer and move a coin around your belt the number of squares you have thrown. When you land on a numbered bag you can collect it, by making a note of its number.

The winner is the first person to collect all their baggage.

Map maze

Mrs Flight is studying a map of the departure lounge she is in, to find the Costa Fortune airport exit. See if you can work out which of the three maps below she is looking at.

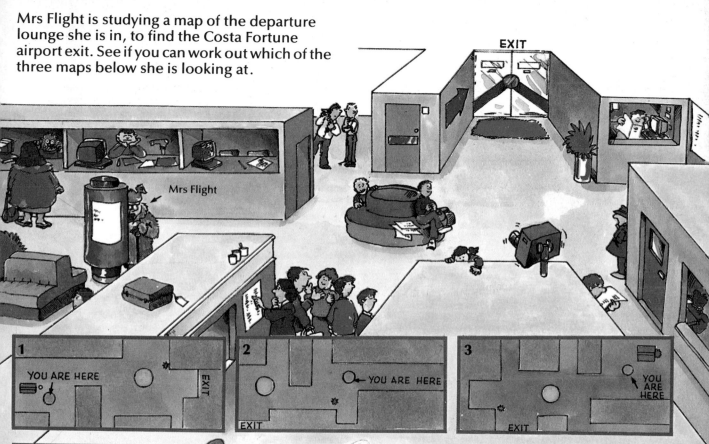

EXIT

Mrs Flight

1
YOU ARE HERE
EXIT

2
YOU ARE HERE
EXIT

3
YOU ARE HERE
EXIT

Change it

When you go abroad you often need to change your money for the money of another country. Mrs Bagsfull wants to change Fogsville splots for Costa Fortune money so that she can shop at the airport. The table below shows what her splots are worth.

How many splots does Mrs Bagsfull need to change into Costa Fortune money to buy all the things in the shop window below?

Fogsville money	Costa Fortune money
10 splots	=	1 zingo
2 splots	=	1 lug

2 lugs

1 zingo

2½ zingos

4 lugs

Make a superstunt plane

This superstunt paper plane can turn right or left, spin or dive. You can make it from a rectangular-shaped piece of paper by following the steps below. The bigger the paper the bigger your plane will be. To launch the plane, grip it underneath the front and throw it slightly downwards. You could use it at home or outdoors.

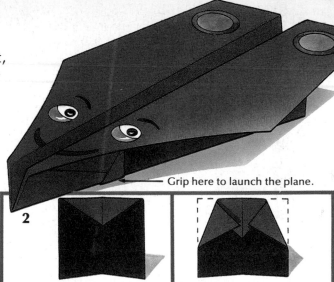

Grip here to launch the plane.

1

Fold the paper in half lengthways.

Flatten the paper out. Fold the top corners down to the centre.

2

Fold the top point downwards as shown above.

Then fold the top corners down to the centre fold line.

3

Fold point A up as shown above.

Fold points B and C to the centre.

Pinch the centre fold together.

4

If you like, decorate your plane with coloured pens or pencils. You could give it a face and badges on the wings.

Stunt tips

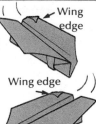

Wing edge

Wing edge

1 Left turn : fold the left wing edge up.

2 Right turn : fold the right wing edge up.

3 Spin : turn the right wing edge up and curve the rudder to the right.

Rudder

4 Dive : fold both the wing edges up.

Did you know?

The record for an outdoor paper plane flight is 2km (1 1/4 miles), set in New York.

60

Captain's log

Aeroplane Captains keep a record of their flights in a logbook. You might like to make your own log in a notebook to record the details of your air journey. The journey log shown below takes up three pages. It is a good idea to prepare the log beforehand, so you can fill it in as you go along.

You could also make a scrapbook on other pages by sticking in things collected on the journey, like baggage labels or ticket stubs. The pictures below show how to divide the pages of your notebook to make the log.

Page 1 — The departure

Airport name	**Fogsville**
Date of journey	**July 27th**
Time of arrival at airport	**8.30 a.m.**
Flight gate number	**5** (This is where you go to board your plane.)

Page 2 — The aeroplane

Flight number	**321** (This will be marked on your ticket.)
Type of plane	**DC10** (Ask a flight attendant.)
Name of airline	**Mugsair**
Seat number	**14** (You will get a boarding pass with a number on it.)

Page 3 — The Flight

Time the flight took	**3 hrs.** (Time the journey from take-off to landing.)
Where it landed	**Costa Fortune** (The name of the airport and country.)
Distance travelled	**500 splats** (Ask a flight attendant.)
What I did on board	**Played air travel games**

Scrapbook pages

Answers

Page 36
Camera clues

The changes in the camera picture are circled below.

Page 37
Let us out!

The crew push a piece of paper partly under the door. They poke the key out of the keyhole with the end of a spoon, so that it falls onto the piece of paper. Then they pull it back under the door.

Whose jacket?

The Captain has the Flight Engineer's jacket. The First Officer has the Captain's jacket. The Flight Engineer has the First Officer's jacket.

Queuing Quickies

Flight 323 is going to Italy. Flight 297 is going to Greece. Flight 345 is going to Egypt. Flight 595 is going to Russia.

Page 38
Smuggler search

Hans Cuffed is disguised as Ian Flight movie

Page 38 (continued)
Passport pieces

A and D don't fit Lady Lollybag's picture.

Page 40
Potty's planes

Number 3 is the only plane without wheels.

Air badges

The Gulf Air badge makes up the fourth pair because it shows a winged creature, like the Lufthansa badge. The other pairs also show pictures which are similar.

Sneaky spies

This is the route James Pond took.

Page 41
Spy catching

The spies are on pages 44, 45, 46, 52 and 59.

Who is it?

Birdman Jack is going to stay with his grandmother.

Page 42

Spot the planes

There is no DC10 at Fogsville, so Peter Perfect's list is the right one.

Page 43

Airport trucks

The scissor platform is missing.

Page 44

Seating plan

James Pond sits in seat 1, Lady Lollybags sits in seat 2, Lotta Trouble sits in seat 3, Peter Perfect sits in seat 4, Rick Ord sits in seat 5 and Mrs Bagsfull sits in seat 6.

A parking problem

Move the planes around in two steps, as shown below.

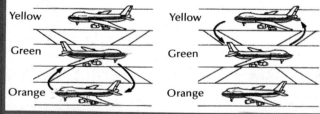

Page 45

Truck mechanic

Hans should mend truck B, because it will take only 50 minutes.

Page 46

The great air quiz

Answers: 1b, 2c, 3a, 4c, 5c, 6b, 7c, 8b, 9a, 10a

Page 47

Air alphabet

Riddle - what has big ears and flies? Answer - a Jumbo.

Air story

The missing word is yankee.

Page 50

Time changes

The towns are shown below.

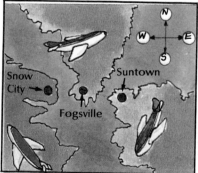

Flying fashion

Jim is wearing Mabel's hat and skirt and Bert's jacket and shoes. Bert is wearing Jim's trousers and hat and Mabel's jacket and shoes. Mabel is wearing Jim's jacket and shoes and Bert's hat and trousers.

Page 52
On autopilot

This is the route the plane takes.

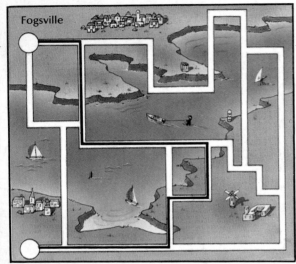

Fogsville

Fancy meeting you

The planes must be the same distance away from Costa Fortune when they pass.

Page 53
Music mimes

Passenger 1 is listening to the Violin Waltz, passenger 2 is listening to Rockin' Drums, passenger 3 is listening to Trumpet Blues and passenger 4 is listening to Guitar Gertie.

Fit the food

Tray 1 belongs to Mrs Flight, tray 2 belongs to D. Racula, tray 3 belongs to Birdman Jack and tray 4 belongs to Ian Trouble.

Page 54
The plane race

The blue plane finishes first at 6.30 p.m., the yellow plane finishes at 6.40 p.m. and the red plane finishes at 7.20 p.m.

Page 55
Air acrobatics

This is how the acrobats made the second pyramid.

Mixed up movie

The correct order of scenes is 5, 1, 4, 3, 6, 2.

Page 57
Marshalling maze

The plane parks at bay 3.

Mystery number

The missing number is 27.

Page 59
Map maze

Mrs Flight is looking at map 3.

Change it

Mrs Bagsfull needs to change 47 splots.

First published in 1986 by Usborne Publishing Ltd, 20 Garrick Street, London WC2E 9BJ, England.
Copyright © 1986 Usborne Publishing Ltd

Printed in Belgium